GRUESOME T... FOR GRUESOME BOYS

Dedicated to my own 3 gruesome boys

Meet the gruesome boys..

in this gruesome book...

GEMPH BOY

His real name was Stan, he was nearly ten years old,

He was skinny as a rake, but he really was quite bold.

He farted all day long, and it brought him so much joy,

And that's why all the kids at school had nicknamed him Gemph Boy!

One day he sat in history class, listening to Miss Claire,

When he pumped a pump so powerful, it blew him off his chair!

The teacher was so angry, she sent him out of class,

But all the kids were choking still, on Gemph Boy's bottom gas!

Soon he was allowed back in, he promised to be smart,

But once again he let one rip – a thunderous smelly fart!

All the children laughed and cheered, "Go Gemph Boy" they all sang,

As his bum–hole fired out air grenades

with...

Now Miss Claire was furious, "You've used up your last chance!

Your trumps are so explosive that they've burnt right through your pants!"

Stan was sent home right away, he knew Dad would be cross,

But Mum's the one he feared the most, as she's the real boss!

She makes him eat his vegetables — carrots, sprouts the lot,

Stan says that's the reason why his bum burps smell like rot!

Mum and Dad got home from work — Stan was feeling scared,

Sat there in his holey pants, his little bum cheeks bared.

"Don't be angry Mummy, please! I only did a trump"

"You've done much more than that, you smelly farty lazy lump!

You've burnt another pair of pants, d'you know how much they cost?

No more treats for you young man, they're gone, finito, lost!"

"That's so unfair!" cried Gemph Boy, "I'm going to run away,

And live somewhere where children rule, and play and fart all day.

We'll never eat our vegetables, wipe our bums or wash,

We'll live off cakes and crisps and sweets — as much as we can nosh!"

Gemph Boy packed a suitcase, and waited until dark,

He crept out of the front door, and headed to the park.

There he sat upon a swing, wondering what to do,

"I'm scared, I miss my Mummy... and now I need a poo!"

Gemph Boy ran home quickly, and crept into his bed,

He thought of all the things he'd done, the silly things he'd said.

"From now on" declared Gemph Boy, "I'll never trump again!"

He kept his word for six whole days, but guess what happened then?

All the farts he'd sucked back in, had stored up in his tum,

"Oh no!" screamed Stan "Oh help me, something's happening in my bum!"

Right then and there a thunderous sound (I tell you it's the truth),

A fart so big came out his bum and shot him through the roof!

They never saw young Stan again, his parents were so sad,

So they wanted me to tell you, that farting's not so bad.

"Never hold it in" they say, "or you might blast off too!

Always push your trumps right out, but careful not to  **poo!"**

HARRY SLATER

– the vegetable hater

Harry is a quiet lad, a dainty little thing,

He doesn't like to play outside, to laugh or dance or sing.

One more major thing to note – a fact that's quite well known,

He's never eaten vegetables – that's why he's never grown!

Harry is at High School now, but still looks like he's five,

I'm not sure how he's still around, and how he's stayed alive.

It started many years ago, when he was only two,

His mummy gave him broccoli – he flushed it down the loo!

Then she gave him carrots, he threw them on the floor,

And then she tried some mushy peas, he flung them out the door!

Every time his mummy tried to feed her son some veg,

He'd launch it out the window and across the garden hedge!

Poor Mum was at her wits end, she couldn't make him eat,

She even tried to bribe him with his very favourite treat!

But that did not work either, he simply wouldn't try,

He'd stomp his feet and punch his fists and shout and scream and cry.

He wouldn't eat tomatoes, sweetcorn, sprouts or swede,

He simply wasn't getting all the vitamins he'd need

To grow up like a big boy, tall and smart and strong,

All he'd eat was chips and cheese, but Mum knew that was wrong.

She cooked up veg in different ways – roasted, sautéed, fried,

But Harry would go mental — as if someone had died!

She hid it in the pasta sauce, but Harry sniffed it out,

She'd blend it with his favourite juice, but he was having nowt!

He'd hide the stuff under his plate, throw it at the wall,

Mum would find it splattered on the floor rug in the hall.

He'd stash it in his toy box, and underneath his bed,

He'd hide it in his school bag, the office or the shed.

His parents got so sick of it, they screamed "This has to stop!"

As Dad was wiping veg soup off the floor with his new mop.

"I'm sick of you not trying, now I'll no longer lie,

If you don't eat your veg young man, I fear that you might die."

Harry was defiant as he threw down fork and knife,

And stomped off up towards his room, protesting "It's my life!"

So Mummy pulled the big guns out and took away his toys,

Then sent him off to live with all the other naughty boys.

So now he lives at boarding school one hundred miles away,

Where he's forced to eat his vegetables — **EVERY SINGLE DAY!**

FOOTCHEESE FRED

In a dingy little bedsit at the end of Bogey Lane,

Lived Foot Cheese Fred, his Mum and Dad, and stinky sister Jane.

They really were revolting in so many different ways,

They wouldn't wash or wipe their bums or clean their teeth for days!

Their home was thick with dirt and grime, and stank of rotten cheese,

The bath was full of cockroaches, the beds were full of fleas!

Now Mum and Dad and sister Jane were horrible and mean,

They picked on Fred and played the meanest pranks you've ever seen!

In fact it was their favourite thing, to torture this poor boy,

To tease or trick or bully him, would bring them so much joy.

They'd use his brand new toothbrush, to clean inside the loo,

Or superglue the toilet seat before his morning poo!

They sprinkled itching powder in his trousers, pants and socks,

They filled his shoes with jam and filled his school bag full of rocks!

They prodded him and poked him, they hid earwigs in his bed,

They tripped him up and stole his food and flicked peas at his head!

One day Fred thought "I've had enough! I'm sick of all these games!

I'm fed up of their tricks and jokes and all the nasty names!

It's time I got my own back – they've all been so unkind"

Just then an evil plan began to creep into his mind.

Now there's something I've not told you, about this young lad Fred,

If you went near his feet and sniffed – you'd likely end up dead.

He'd wear the same old stinky socks for ten days in a row,

Which hid the sticky lumps of cheese between each dirty toe.

So Fred peeled off his smelly socks and took his mum's cheese grater,

And filed the hard skin off his heels til' half an hour later

He'd made a quite impressive pile of stinky yellow stuff,

Made up of gooey foot cheese, hard skin, toenails and toe fluff.

He hid this bowl of stenchy stuff right underneath his bed,

And went over his grotesque plan (just once more) in his head.

The next day it was Friday which meant horrid old Aunt Betty,

Would come round for her tea which was tinned meatballs and spaghetti.

As they sat down on the sofa with their bowls upon their knees,

Young Fred jumped up and said "Hang on, I'll go and fetch the cheese!"

He sneaked into his room and reaching underneath his bed,

He grabbed the plate of foot cheese (which he'd give to them instead!)

Fred tried not to giggle, as he perched upon the settee,

And watched as his whole family sprinkled 'cheese' on their spaghetti.

His mum was first to comment "My this cheese is appetising,

It's melting in my mouth, it's really scrumptious and surprising."

Dad slurped up his dinner (dribbling sauce all down his chin),

"It certainly is strong my dear" he muttered with a grin.

Stinky sister Jane (to Fred's surprise) was very keen,

She guzzled up her food and started licking her bowl clean.

Horrid Old Aunt Betty laughed and (rubbing at her tummy),

Belched a great big burp and said "Now wasn't that just yummy?!"

Pretty soon the food was gone – the bowls and cheese plate bare,

"Ha ha you rotten lot" said Fred "I'm happy to declare –

You've all just eaten footcheese from my stinky smelly feet"

He rubbed his hands together as he sighed "Revenge is sweet"

BIG BULLY BURT

Trumpton Hill School was a lovely little school, at the bottom of a very steep hill,

The teachers were all caring and the children were so friendly, and no one was unhappy UNTIL...

The day Big Bully Burt started halfway through year three, when his family moved in just across the street,

He was bigger than the other kids and towered way above them, and he had enormous spades for hands and feet.

On his first day he announced that as of now he was the boss, and his classmates should do everything he said,

And if they didn't listen and obey his cruel commands, they would get a great big slap around the head.

From that day on the children would endeavour to avoid him,
ensuring they all stayed out of his way,

But Burt was sure to find them as they went about their
business, determined he would sabotage their play.

He chased the little girls and he pulled their pretty pigtails,
and threw their favourite dollies in the mud,

He terrorised the boys, tied their shoelaces together, and he
laughed as they fell over with a thud.

He demanded all the pupils should hand over their packed
lunches, and do all of his rotten homework too,

And if they disagreed or if they went to tell a teacher, he would
flush their brainy heads right down the loo.

It was near the end of term and the children were surprised,
when another new child registered in class,

She was confident and friendly and seemed pretty clever too,
and had just about the right amount of sass.

Burt sat right behind her and throughout their morning lessons,
he annoyed the girl by kicking at her chair,

And right before the bell he took his scissors and leant forward,
and he cut the brand new ribbons in her hair.

At playtime all the children warned the new girl all about him, and
advised her to avoid him if she could,

But just as they were talking and devouring their cheese sarnies,
Bully Burt was heading right for where they stood!

As he reached the crowd of children he demanded they
relinquish all their dinner money, chocolate, crisps and
drinks,

When the new girl she stepped forward with her
hands upon her hips, and declared "Hey Burt,
your attitude – IT STINKS!"

Burt turned crimson red and he was
frothing at the mouth, as he turned
to push the girl (whose name was
Rose),

But Rose was quick and fierce,
as she pulled her right arm
back, and with all her might she
punched him on the nose!

"You don't scare me you bully, you are nothing but a coward, and I certainly won't stand for all your games!

I'll let no one bully me, steal my lunch or cut my ribbons, push my friends and call them horrid, hurtful names!"

Burt's lip began to tremble then he started sobbing loudly, "My nose is bleeding! Help! I want my Mum!"

He turned around to run away but just for added measure Rose delivered him a swift kick up the bum.

He found the Dinner Lady and he held onto her apron as he pleaded "Help me please, my nose, it hurts!"

"It serves you right young man" she said "You always had it coming and you've only gone and got your just desserts."

All the children cheered as they gathered round the new girl, "Hooray!" they said "You really were so brave!"

But all it really took was someone bold enough to challenge him, and now (you mark my words) Burt will behave.

EARWAX EDDIE

Sit down my friend now are you ready

To hear the tale of Earwax Eddie,

Whose ears were full of dirt and grime

And hairy mushrooms, scabs and slime!

It came in handy all that wax

For tasty little morning snacks.

He'd have a poke and rummage round

Until a filthy treat was found.

He'd pull it out with his long finger

And on his tongue he'd let it linger.

The snot–like treat would melt quite slow

Then down his food pipe it would go.

One day young Ed was sat in school

Behind his desk upon his stool.

He rummaged deep inside his lug,

He felt a blob and gave a tug.

He started pulling something out,

His classmate Poppy gave a shout!

For out his ear a long green thing

Was stretching out like gooey string!

Eddie slowly pulled and tugged

And out this slug—like matter slugged.

By now the class had gathered round,

The slug so long it reached the ground!

And Eddie just kept right on tugging,

The gooey mollusk kept on slugging,

Heaping slime upon the floor,

Alas now Ed could pull no more.

He'd pulled his brains out of his head

And with a thud he dropped down

dead!

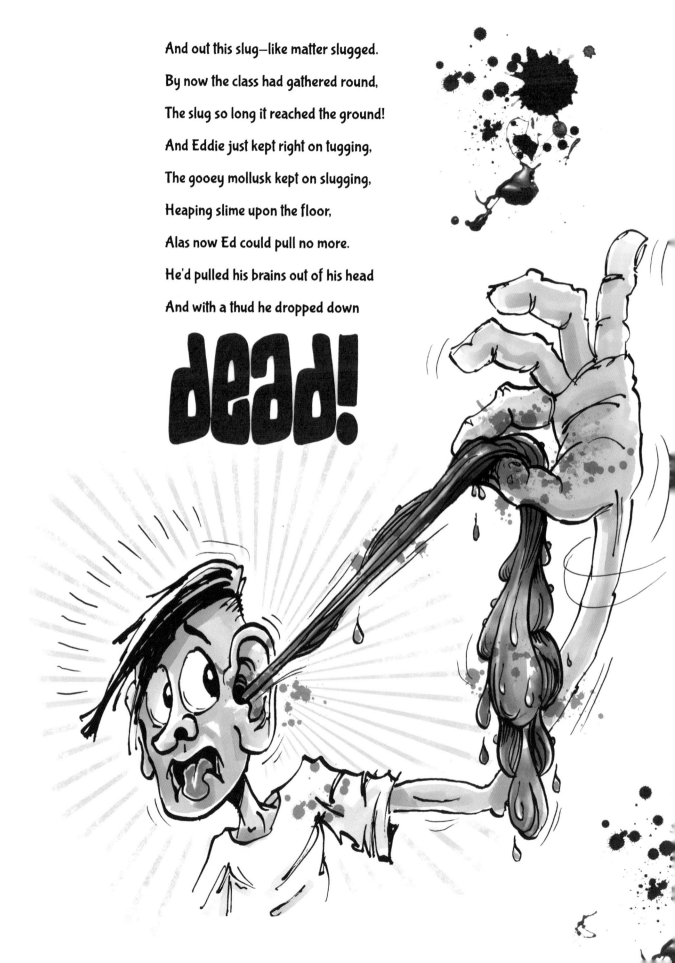

STINKY BABY SISTER

As I sat down to eat my tea,

Mum said "Come sit down next to me.

We've got exciting news to tell!"

I looked at Dad who grinned as well.

"We're going to have another baby!"

"Whatever — can you pass the gravy?"

"Well aren't you pleased?" replied my dad,

Who also seemed a little mad.

Mum looked sad and rubbed her belly,

I groaned "Can't I just watch the telly?"

A few months passed and mum got fatter,

What I thought seemed not to matter.

I didn't want a smelly sibling,

Screaming, crying, pooping, dribbling.

The day arrived, I heard Mum shout

"I think the baby's coming out!"

Dad ran off to start the car

And I was left with old Grandma.

Next day – as I lounged on the floor,

Mum and Dad burst through the door,

"We're home" they cried "We've had a girl!

A perfect gem, we'll call her Pearl."

Mum cooed "Oh she's such a doll."

I said "She looks more like a troll!

I just don't want a baby sister"

Dad said "Come on calm down Mister"

"No!" I cried "Why can't you see?

There's only enough love for me?"

And up I got and stomped away,

Where in my room I'd spend the day.

So that was it, life as I knew it

Was over (how would I get through it?)

I grabbed some paper and a pen,

I racked my little brains and then

Oh yes that's it! By Jove by Jack!

We need to send the baby back!

I'll write the stork a pleading letter

And hopefully he'll come and get her!

I'll have a toy sale in the yard

And sell her off, it won't be hard.

I'll price her right, say one pound ten,

Someone's sure to buy her then!

If not I'll put her in a crate,

Affix a stamp, Address: Kuwait.

And failing that I'll stick her in

The green or brown recycle bin!

I'll put her out with all the litter,

I'm sure Mum won't be all that bitter!

My parents will then surely see

There's only room enough for me!

PIZZA PETE

My name is Pete and I will ONLY eat pizza!

Pizza for breakfast, pizza for snack

In the front yard or hanging out back

Pizza for lunch, pizza for tea

Sat at the table or plonked on my knee

Pizza for picnics and in my packed lunch

Pizza at snack time, elevenses or brunch

Pizza for supper, pizza in bed

Pizza with movies and blanket and ted

Pizza when happy, joyful or glad

Pizza when gloomy, moody or sad

Pizza whilst showering or sat in the bath

Pizza whilst riding my bike on the path

Pizza at school in the middle of class

Pizza whilst sunbathing laid on the grass

Pizza whilst swimming or out in the park

Pizza in daylight or when it gets dark

Pizza at Nan's house or sat on a plane

Pizza when sunny or drizzling with rain

Pizza on holiday, pizza at home

Pizza in London or Paris or Rome

Pizza for birthdays and special occasions

Pizza whilst doing my homework equations

Pizza at Christmas (no turkey for me)

Pizza with cream cakes at afternoon tea

Pizza whilst playing games on my computer

Pizza whilst practising tricks on my scooter

Pizza served hot, or cold the next morning

Pizza when lively or sleepy and yawning

Pizza at home or when I'm out shopping

Pizza with ABSOLUTELY ANY TOPPING

SUCH AS....

Pizza with onions, pizza with cheese

Pizza with raspberries and honey from bees

Pizza with mushrooms and sardines and ham

Pizza with peppers and olives and jam

Pizza with pineapple, swiss cheese or feta

Pizza with corned beef, tomatoes, pancetta

Pizza with prawns or Italian meat

Spicy and fiery or sour or sweet

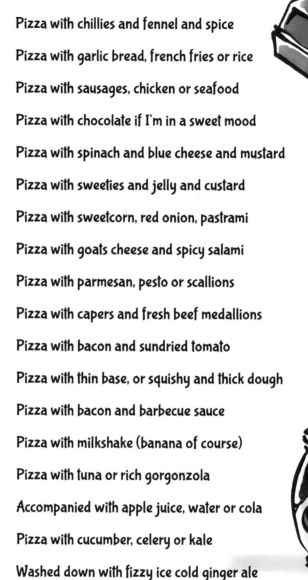

Pizza with chillies and fennel and spice

Pizza with garlic bread, french fries or rice

Pizza with sausages, chicken or seafood

Pizza with chocolate if I'm in a sweet mood

Pizza with spinach and blue cheese and mustard

Pizza with sweeties and jelly and custard

Pizza with sweetcorn, red onion, pastrami

Pizza with goats cheese and spicy salami

Pizza with parmesan, pesto or scallions

Pizza with capers and fresh beef medallions

Pizza with bacon and sundried tomato

Pizza with thin base, or squishy and thick dough

Pizza with bacon and barbecue sauce

Pizza with milkshake (banana of course)

Pizza with tuna or rich gorgonzola

Accompanied with apple juice, water or cola

Pizza with cucumber, celery or kale

Washed down with fizzy ice cold ginger ale

Pizza with brie, avocado or shrimps

Pizza with hot jalapenos (*no wimps*)

I'll eat pizza with

ABSOLUTELY
ANYTHING!

MEAT EATER MARVIN

Marvin was a strapping lad, nearly five foot two,

His favourite sport was eating meat, as much as he could chew.

From bacon, beef and turkey, to rabbit, lamb and pheasant,

Pork and ham and juicy steak and goat (which he found pleasant).

Sausages and goose and duck, offal, ribs and rind,

Chicken, ostrich, kangaroo — whatever he could find!

He'd scoff it any way he could — with mustard, gravy, fries,

With veg and spuds and yorkshire puds, in sandwiches, in pies.

Roasted, barbecued, pan—fried, cooked well done or rare,

Griddled, sizzled, stir—fried, boiled or grilled — he didn't care.

Liver, kidneys, heart and lungs — he'd gobble up the lot,

He'd suck the flesh clean off the bones then boil them in a pot.

His mind was always thinking, when he'd next be fed,

He'd see a sheep and think "You'd do — between two hunks of bread!

Accompanied with relish, blackberry coulis or mint jelly,

Or any kind of condiment, so long's you're in my belly!"

His mother tried to warn him he should cut down on the meat,

Marv scoffed "Without these animals what else is there to eat?"

"Try some pasta Marv my boy, fruit and veg or rice...

...potatoes, salad, lentils, nuts and grains — they would be nice!"

"I won't touch all that rubbish Mum, gosh I'm not a snail...

I won't eat lettuce, grapes, tomatoes, celery or kale!"

Grabbing his mum's roasting pan, the boy threw in a lamb,

He flavoured it with salt and closed the oven with a slam.

Once cooked he sat down quite prepared to chomp his juicy feast,

But from his plate ALAS! there rose a horrifying beast!

The lamb was taking form of a most terrifying shape,

Marv shrank down into his chair, and stared — his mouth agape.

The creature stretched up off the plate with teeth and arms and eyes,

Marv's mum was busy hoovering — she couldn't hear the cries.

The frightened boy could barely speak, but motioned with his knife,

"I—Is this really happening — have you really come to life?"

The creature leaned towards him, dripping with mint sauce,

"You've eaten half my family, I hope you feel remorse!

How'd you think you'd feel you brute, if the tables turned?

If you were basted, grilled or fried or sautéed, roasted, burned?"

With that he lunged towards the boy, cackling with glee,

"So now instead I'm going to gobble YOU up for my tea!"

"No!" cried Marv "I beg of you — have mercy on my soul!"

"Too late" cried lamb "I'm starving" and he swallowed young Marv whole.

Twas nothing left of Marvin (now he'd met his fate),

All his mother found was his school tie upon his plate.

DIRTY DEXTER

The mums and teachers at the school,

All shared one big important rule.

All children should be washed and bathed

And courteous and well—behaved.

But there was one who didn't seem

To scrub up well or shine or gleam.

His name was Dexter Honeywell,

And boy did this kid really smell!

But much to Teacher's raging wrath,

He just refused to take a bath!

His mother hoped it was a phase,

But it had lasted ninety days.

She tried all sorts to bribe her child,

But this would only get him riled.

She tempted him with sweets and chocs

"At least just change your pants and socks!"

But still the lad would not give in,

Despite his dirt—encrusted skin,

The muck was thick and so ingrained,

His fingernails unkempt and stained.

His hair was foul and crawled with nits

And mushrooms sprouted in his pits.

Behind his ears lay grime so thick,

Enough to make his classmates sick.

Yet Dex seemed happy and upbeat,

Unbothered by his stinky feet.

Sat down at home his mother stewed,

How could she end this bath time feud?

"I'm so exhausted with this tosh...

I just can't get the kid to wash!"

But then she got it – "YES!" she cried

"There IS one thing I haven't tried!

I'll send him round to Granny Brine

And she'll soon whip him into line"

For Dexter's Gran (now slightly barmy),

Had served five decades in the army.

At 6 foot 4 and in command,

With leather drill cane in her hand,

And army boots on mammoth feet,

She'd frighten any folk she'd meet!

Now Granny always smelled of bleach,

Barked orders with a deafening screech.

Famous for her tough, strict rules,

She wouldn't gladly suffer fools.

It's well known that, throughout the years,

She'd pushed grown men to floods of tears.

And anyone who was half canny,

Would know to never mess with Granny.

If anyone knocked at her door,

They'd soon experience her roar.

And anyone caught trick or treating,

Could guarantee they'd get a beating.

She'd chase the kids off down the street,

Her drill cane whipping at their feet.

So at the weekend, off Dex hurried,

Suitcase packed and feeling worried.

He didn't dare to show up late,

For that would make the hag irate.

He'd begged his mum "Don't make me go!

It's possible I'll die you know!"

And just the thought of Granny Brine,

Would send a shiver up his spine.

But mum held firm and stood her ground,

She grabbed her coat and drove him round.

Old Gran was waiting in the yard,

Expression fixed and cold and hard.

At once she ordered scared young Dex

To strip down to his under—keks.

"Wait what?!" screamed Dex "We're in the garden!"

"Don't say WHAT young man say PARDON!"

So now amongst the pots and plants,

Dex shivered in his underpants!

Gran turned on the garden hose

And blasted water at his toes,

Then on his legs and then his belly

"Serves you right for being so smelly!"

She aimed it at his arms and back,

And sprayed it in his bottom crack.

The water blasted icy cold,

Shattering the grime and mould,

Then with a sweeping brush Gran rubbed

And washed his skin and doused and scrubbed.

His nails were trimmed, his hair was chopped,

His feet were sponged, his face was mopped.

His ears were flushed, his teeth were steamed,

Soon every bit of Dexter gleamed!

So home he went all nice and clean,

A positively different teen.

Now without fail young Dexter scours

His body during daily showers,

And reeling from the aftermath,

He won't refuse his Sunday bath.

Thank you for reading Gruesome Tales For Gruesome Boys! If you enjoyed the book and have a moment to spare, please do leave a short review on Amazon and/or social media. Your help spreading the word about these gruesome boys would be very much appreciated

Fran Grant – Author

Fran Grant is an author and bookworm. She lives in Yorkshire with her husband and three gruesome little boys.

Facebook @frangrantwriter

Instagram @fran_grant_writer

Website www.frangrant.com

Dave is probably 'THE BEST ILLUSTRATOR IN THE WORLD... well, he's not bad. The original gruesome 'scribbling boy', who splodged ink and paint everywhere he went!

Dave Bull – Illustrator

Dave lives and works in the North of England with three gruesome dogs. A time traveller in his spare time.

Website www.davebull.co.uk

4x table

1 × 4 = 4
2 × 4 = 8
3 × 4 = 12
4 × 4 = 16
5 × 4 = 20
6 × 4 = 24
7 × 4 = 28
8 × 4 = 32
9 × 4 = 36
10 × 4 = 40
11 × 4 = 44
12 × 4 = 48

5x table

1 × 5 = 5
2 × 5 = 10
3 × 5 = 15
4 × 5 = 20
5 × 5 = 25
6 × 5 = 30
7 × 5 = 35
8 × 5 = 40
9 × 5 = 45
10 × 5 = 50
11 × 5 = 55
12 × 5 = 60

6x table

1 × 6 = 6
2 × 6 = 12
3 × 6 = 18
4 × 6 = 24
5 × 6 = 30
6 × 6 = 36
7 × 6 = 42
8 × 6 = 48
9 × 6 = 54
10 × 6 = 60
11 × 6 = 66
12 × 6 = 72

10x table

1 × 10 = 10
2 × 10 = 20
3 × 10 = 30
4 × 10 = 40
5 × 10 = 50
6 × 10 = 60
7 × 10 = 70
8 × 10 = 80
9 × 10 = 90
10 × 10 = 100
11 × 10 = 110
12 × 10 = 120

11x table

1 × 11 = 11
2 × 11 = 22
3 × 11 = 33
4 × 11 = 44
5 × 11 = 55
6 × 11 = 66
7 × 11 = 77
8 × 11 = 88
9 × 11 = 99
10 × 11 = 110
11 × 11 = 121
12 × 11 = 132

12x table

1 × 12 = 12
2 × 12 = 24
3 × 12 = 36
4 × 12 = 48
5 × 12 = 60
6 × 12 = 72
7 × 12 = 84
8 × 12 = 96
9 × 12 = 108
10 × 12 = 120
11 × 12 = 132
12 × 12 = 144

Printed in Great Britain
by Amazon